Sol

La

Ti

The Other Do

Notso Profundo

A Noteworthy Tale

For Mason
and all the children

For Tom

By Brenda Mutchnick and Ron Casden   Illustrated by Ian Penney

HARRY N. ABRAMS, INC., PUBLISHERS

Notso Profundo woke up singing—but then, *everyone* in Rhapsody wakes up singing. That's because Rhapsody is the magical place where all music is created. It's also the home of Do, Re, Mi, Fa, Sol, La, Ti, and The Other Do—the eight Notes of the musical scale.

The secret way into Rhapsody is locked inside the key of the scale called "C." As each note is sung, it becomes the step of a staircase which leads up to Rhapsody. It will only work, however, if you are standing in a forest, a field of green, or even next to a single flower. Notso Profundo has the only key.

For as long as anyone could remember, Notso had taken care of the Notes. And for as long as Notso could remember, it hadn't been an easy job. Do, Re, Mi, Fa, Sol, La, Ti, and The Other Do were as different in sight as they were in sound. One was classy. One was sassy. Two were taller. One was smaller. One was shaped just like a fiddle. One was always stuck in the middle. And the one who worried was easy to see. Look around. It would always be Mi.

Notso owned the Notable Inn, where all the Notes lived. And he was the Guardian of the Grand Baton, which he used every morning to start the new day. The Notes waited patiently for Notso to give the signal to play.

The Festival of Rhythm and Rhyme was less than two days away. This was Rhapsody's biggest celebration. Everyone was very excited. Notso raised the Grand Baton so fast that it flew right out of his hands. It bounced once, then twice, then off the balcony and into The Groove, a swiftly moving creek that flowed past the Notable Inn.

Notso chased after the Grand Baton. He followed as it floated in the water down through Hello Hollow, around The Waltzing Woods, over Fiddle Falls, and in between the Rocks that Roll. Suddenly, The Groove flowed underground.

Taking a deep breath, Notso closed his eyes, held his nose, and jumped in. He was twirled and swirled, tumbled and hurled. Suddenly, The Groove turned into a long waterfall. THUD! Notso hit bottom. THUD! The Grand Baton hit his head.

Notso was wet. He was tired. He was LOST. He had never been this far away from the Notable Inn. In fact, he wasn't even in Rhapsody anymore. There were no trees. No grass. No birds. No color. And—no music. A big sign read: **ENTERING SLURRRR. GO AWAY**. That's fine with me, he thought. He started looking for a forest, a field of green—or just one flower—so he could use his key of "C" and get back up to Rhapsody.

The buildings were so tall and close together that he could not see the sky. Everywhere signs read **NO MUSIC! NO HUMMING! WHISTLING IS NOT ALLOWED! DO NOT TAP IN RHYTHM! NEVER SING!**

In the middle loomed a giant statue of the meanest-looking man Notso had ever seen—Konrad Troubleclef. Without thinking, Notso began tapping out a little tune with his Baton. He didn't notice the Soundcatcher, hiding behind the statue, who snatched his melody right out of the air. The Soundcatcher stuffed it into his sack and then stuffed Notso into it, too. Notso was dragged down a flight of stairs and dumped at the feet of the real Konrad Troubleclef.

DO NOT TAP
IN RHYTHM

Notso stood up and started to speak, but Konrad yelled "Silence! You're under arrest for breaking the no music law." He told the Soundcatcher to lock Notso up.

"Wait," Notso said, "There must be some mistake. Music is a way of life where I come from. In Rhapsody…" Konrad interrupted. "Rhapsody? The one where Do, Re, Mi, Fa, Sol, La, Ti, and The Other Do live? *That* Rhapsody?" "Yes, and I am the one in charge of them," Notso answered. Konrad's voice suddenly softened. "Well, young man, that's quite an important job. Now what if something happened to one of your Notes?"

Notso had never even thought about such a terrible thing. "My goodness," he said, "I guess music would just stop... EVERYWHERE."

Konrad smiled wickedly. He had always wanted to put an end to music everywhere, and now he had a plan. "Do come and spend the night in my castle," he coaxed. "You must be tired and hungry. I'll give you a good dinner and a warm place to sleep." Notso was so tired he could hardly keep his eyes open, so he agreed.

They went to Konrad's castle, but instead of food and a cozy bed, Notso was led down, down, down a dark staircase into a dungeon and locked into a very big cage. There, inside the cage, was the most beautiful girl he had ever seen.

"Who are you?" Notso whispered, afraid that she would vanish like a dream. "My name is Melisma Tone-Cluster. Konrad Troubleclef is holding me prisoner until I agree to marry him. But I'd rather spend the rest of my life locked in this cage!"

Notso told her all about his horrible day, and that he, too, would rather spend the rest of his life in a cage than tell Konrad about the secret way into Rhapsody.

Meanwhile, Konrad and the Soundcatcher were meeting in a hidden private chamber. Konrad opened a small door high in the wall and carefully took out a mysteriously glowing Black Box. The Soundcatcher cracked open his bag. At the same time, Konrad barely opened the Box.

For a moment, every kind of music imaginable filled the air. Quickly, the Soundcatcher slid Notso's melody into the Box and slammed it shut.

This is where Konrad had hidden all the music that belonged in Slurrrr.

"Now," Konrad said, "You must find the way into Rhapsody, steal one of the Notes, and bring it back to me." The Soundcatcher, who couldn't speak because he had once, by accident, caught his own voice, eagerly nodded yes. "Go hide near Notso's cage and listen carefully. Maybe you'll hear the secret. Meanwhile, I'm going to have my dinner."

Poor Rose Transpose, Konrad's devoted housekeeper, had always wanted to marry him. She was kind and very polite. But there was one problem. No matter how hard she tried, everything got mixed up. Now, she was making Konrad breakfast for dinner, carefully scrambling his toast and spreading jam on his eggs. Rose was heating up a fresh pot of orange juice when Konrad burst in.

He told Rose that he was going to marry Melisma in the morning—whether Melisma agreed to it or not.

Poor, poor, Rose. She really thought *she* should be the next Mrs. Troubleclef. So after Konrad had gone to bed, she crept down to the dungeon and opened the cage.

She told Melisma to run, that Konrad planned to marry her tomorrow. Rose wasn't sure why, but she thought it had to do with Konrad getting a letter, or note, from some place called Rap City. In fact, the Soundcatcher was on his way to pick it up.

Notso jumped to his feet. Do, Re, Mi, Fa, Sol, La, Ti, and The Other Do were in danger. He had to get back to Rhapsody. But how?

Not knowing that the Soundcatcher was listening, Notso told Rose that he needed to find a forest, a field of green, or just a single flower.

Rose said, "Follow me."

There, on the roof of Konrad's castle, Rose showed them her garden. It was really just some green spots on old potatoes that were spoiling— but it *was* "green."

Notso took Melisma's hand, and with his key of "C" played the first Do. A stair appeared before them. He played Re and another stair appeared. And another, and another, until they climbed through the clouds. They never looked back, or they would have seen the Soundcatcher following behind them.

When they reached The Other Do, Melisma got her first look at Rhapsody. There were colors she had never imagined. She heard sounds she had never heard. And she felt happier than she had ever been in her whole life. They ran all the way to the Notable Inn.

All the Notes were safe and sound, and glad that Notso was home. They wanted to know where he had been and who was this beautiful girl?

Notso told them the whole story.

The Notes could tell right away that Melisma was someone very special. They couldn't wait to show her the magic of music.

They went inside an empty room.
There were no pictures.
No lights. No chairs.
Then the Notes
joined hands
and now
Melisma saw
the magic.
Do, Re,
Mi, Fa, Sol,
La, Ti, and
The Other Do
started spinning
around until all
she could see was
a rainbow of color.
Melisma heard the
faint sounds of music
in the air.

Her tattered gray dress turned into a sparkling ball gown. Suddenly the room filled with riches. Notso, looking as handsome as a Prince, took her hand and they began to waltz. When the dance ended, all the beautiful things disappeared and the Notes slowly formed their circle and began to spin once again until only the colors of the rainbow were left.

Notso was still worried about the Soundcatcher. He set out to warn the people of Rhapsody to watch out for a little gray man with very big hands.

While Notso was out, Do, Re, Mi, Fa, Sol, La, Ti, and The Other Do all agreed that they would give Melisma a present—they would get her a music box.

When it came time to decide who should pick out the gift, each Note yelled out "me." Thinking they all meant him, Mi jumped up and ran out the door.

Mi spent so long choosing the gift, he decided to take a shortcut home through Piccolo Pines. He stopped a moment to make sure that the music box was wound up, because he wanted it to begin playing as soon as Melisma opened it.

He was listening to his favorite song when the little gray man with very big hands jumped out from behind a tree and scooped him into his sack.

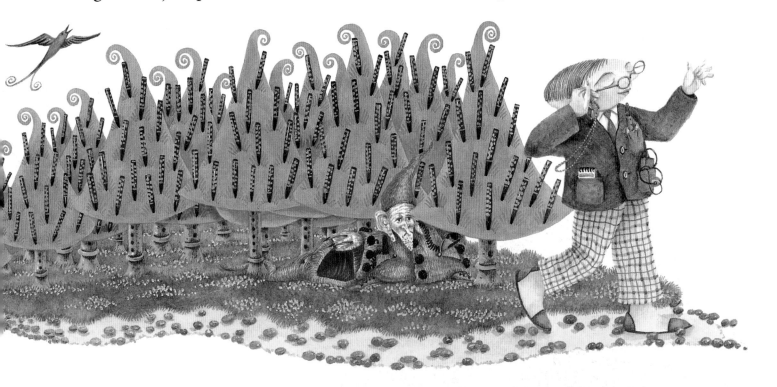

When Notso returned to the Notable Inn, everything was in a terrible mess! MI WAS MISSING! The Festival of Rhythm and Rhyme was to begin the very next day, and now there could be no music! Suddenly, a rock came flying through the window with a message attached:

To the people of Rhapsody:

I have Mi

You have Melisma

You want Mi

I want Melisma

Send her back. If she's not here in the morning, you will never see Mi again

Konrad Troubleclef

Melisma's eyes filled with tears. She did not mean to cause
all this trouble. As soon as everyone was asleep, she
quietly kissed the Notes good-bye, slipped out
of the Notable Inn, and made her
way back to Slurrrr.

Konrad told Rose to prepare Melisma for the wedding, which would take place that very day. After Rose and Melisma left the room, Konrad ordered the Soundcatcher to get rid of Mi as soon as Melisma said "I do."

While Rose brushed Melisma's beautiful long hair, they both heard a strange sound coming from the window.

Rose and Melisma ran over to the balcony, and stared right into the eyes of what they thought was the tallest woman in the world. Melisma shrieked in delight when she recognized The Other Do.

She was standing on Ti, who was standing on La, who was standing on Sol, who was standing on Fa, who was standing on Re, who was standing on Do—and they were all standing on Notso.

Once inside, Melisma hugged each of the Notes. "Where is Mi?" she asked. "Konrad should have freed him by now. He promised."

"Konrad will never let Mi go," Notso said, "And I will never let you marry him." Everyone was in great danger. Notso quickly explained his plan.

Notso and the Notes ran down, down, down the stairs to the cage, where the Soundcatcher was standing guard. The Notes all scattered and started singing. The Soundcatcher didn't know which way to run first. Music was coming from every direction. He stood there frozen and held his ears. Meanwhile, Notso grabbed the keys and freed Mi.

"Are you all right?" Notso asked, but Mi just shook his head and pointed to his throat. Tears were streaming down his face.

Notso grabbed the Soundcatcher and said: "I want Mi's voice and I want it NOW! And if you will help me, I'll get your voice back, too.

The Soundcatcher looked up and smiled for the first time in a very, very long time. He showed Notso the hidden private chamber with the small door high in the wall.

Konrad ordered all of the people of Slurrrr to come to his wedding—and to bring good presents.

When the Preacher pronounced them man and wife, Konrad closed his eyes, lifted the veil, puckered up his lips, and kissed his new bride. When he opened his eyes, imagine his surprise! He had just married Rose Transpose.

Konrad turned around. There were Notso, Melisma, Do, Re, Mi, Fa, Sol, La, Ti, and The Other Do all laughing at the trick they had played on him.

Notso opened the Black Box and music filled the air. Color returned to the land of Slurrrr. Flowers bloomed and grasses grew. Birds sang and the sun came out from behind the clouds. People started dancing in the streets. Even Konrad smiled as he took Rose's hand.

Notso invited all the people of Slurrrr to come to Rhapsody for the Festival of Rhythm and Rhyme. The Notes got in order and sang their way up the magical staircase.

It was the morning of the Festival in Rhapsody. The Notes were dressed in their finest. Everyone had gathered on the lawn of The Notable Inn.

Melisma stepped into the sun. She was glowing in her golden gown of silk and brightly colored ribbons. On her head she wore a crown of fresh flowers, and around her neck was the tiny music box that the Notes had given her so she would never be without music again.

The Notes began to play the Wedding March.

BRENDA MUTCHNICK and RON CASDEN
live on neighboring hills on the outskirts of Slurrrr
where they work for Konrad Troubleclef in the
entertainment industry. Both Brenda and Ron
secretly keep plants in their homes.

IAN PENNEY, illustrator of Abrams' *Ian Penney's
Book of Nursery Rhymes* and *Ian Penney's Book of
Fairy Tales*, resides in Rhapsody with his wife and
two children.

A Noteworthy Tale was inspired by ROBERT
LOSTUTTER, a close personal friend of The Notes,
who lives in Hello Hollow with Theo and Scooter.

Project Director: Margaret L. Kaplan
Design: Christine Cava, Dyer/Mutchnick Group, Inc.

Library of Congress Catalog Card Number: 97–70933
ISBN 0–8109–1386–0

Illustrations copyright © 1997 Ian Penney
Text copyright © 1997 Brenda Mutchnick and Ron Casden

Published in 1997 by Harry N. Abrams, Incorporated, New York

Printed and bound in Hong Kong

Harry N. Abrams, Inc.
100 Fifth Avenue
New York, N.Y. 10011
www.abramsbooks.com